D0359544

*E*xuberant **Jo March** never sits still. Whether she's running races with boys or scribbling and acting in her latest play, Jo is always active and creative. So when Aunt March asks her to befriend Pauline Wheeler, Jo can't believe that the girl spends every day cooped up in her bedroom. True, Pauline is blind and utterly dependent on her governess, but her fear of life exhausts Jo's patience. The two girls simply have nothing in common—until they're caught in a snow squall that changes their lives forever.

PORTRAITS
of LITTLE WOMEN

*Jo Makes
a Friend*

Don't miss any of the
Portraits of Little Women

PORTRAITS
of LITTLE WOMEN

*Jo Makes
a Friend*

Susan Beth Pfeffer

DELACORTE PRESS

Published by
Delacorte Press
Bantam Doubleday Dell Publishing Group, Inc.
1540 Broadway
New York, New York 10036

Copyright © 1998 by Susan Beth Pfeffer

All rights reserved. No part of this book may be reproduced or
transmitted in any form or by any means, electronic or mechanical,
including photocopying, recording, or by any information storage and
retrieval system, without the written permission of the Publisher, except
where permitted by law.

The trademark Delacorte Press® is registered in the U.S. Patent and
Trademark Office and in other countries.

Library of Congress Cataloging-in-Publication Data

Pfeffer, Susan Beth.
    Portraits of Little women, Jo makes a friend / Susan Beth Pfeffer.
        p.   cm.
    "Inspired by Louisa May Alcott's Little women."
    Summary: At the request of her great-aunt, ten-year-old Jo tries to
befriend a sad and lonely blind girl who is visiting the neighborhood.
    ISBN 0-385-32581-9
    [1. Blind—Fiction.   2. Physically handicapped—Fiction.
3. Sisters—Fiction.   4. Family life—New England—Fiction.   5. New
England—Fiction.]   I. Alcott, Louisa May, 1832–1888.   Little women.
II. Title.
PZ7.P44855P jf   1998
[Fic]—dc21   97-49509
                                                                        CIP
                                                                         AC

The text of this book is set in 13-point Cochin.

Cover and text design by Patrice Sheridan
Cover illustration copyright © 1998 by Lori Earley
Text illustrations copyright © 1998 by Marcy Ramsey
Activities illustrations copyright © 1998 by Laura Maestro

Manufactured in the United States of America

July 1998

10   9   8   7   6   5   4   3   2   1

BVG

FOR RUTH SCHWARTZ

LIBRARY
DEXTER SCHOOLS
DEXTER, NM 88230

CONTENTS

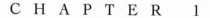

" *J* osephine! Josephine March!"

Jo March stared down at her writing desk and sighed. Only one person ever called her Josephine, and only one person used that demanding tone with her—Aunt March. And when Aunt March called, Jo knew she had to reply.

But Jo felt it was unfair of Aunt March to summon her from her own attic, when she was working so hard to finish her best play ever, *The Curse of Montevideo*. No one would dare interrupt Aunt March when she was working on something. Not that Jo was sure what Aunt

March ever worked at, except making Jo's life miserable.

"Josephine March! Come down at once!"

"Jo, dearest, please come down."

The second voice was Marmee's, and Jo knew how reluctant Marmee always was to disturb her. Marmee had great respect for Jo's writing. So it had to be something important.

"I'm coming," Jo called. She wiped her pen, still dripping with ink (as the Count of Montevideo was dripping with blood), and a bit of the ink got on her sleeve. Jo shook her head. She wore an old pinafore when she wrote, precisely to keep the ink off her clothes. She knew that her dress would be handed down next to her younger sister Beth, and then to her youngest sister, Amy, just as that same dress had been handed down to Jo from her older sister, Meg. But no matter how hard Jo tried to be careful, the ink always seemed to find a place to stain her clothing.

And Aunt March would be sure to notice. Not that she would do anything about it, such as offer to buy new dresses for Beth and

Amy. Simple disapproval would do for Aunt March.

It was so unfair, Jo thought. If only Aunt March had chosen a different day to pay a call on Marmee. Jo walked down the attic stairs and peeked into her bedroom. Meg was sitting silently, working on her embroidery. Beth and Amy were by her side. Beth was dressing one of her dolls, and Amy was sketching.

"We're being quiet as mice," Meg whispered. "Maybe Aunt March won't realize we're here."

"It won't work," Jo whispered back glumly. "She found me, and I was in the attic."

Jo's sisters laughed, not the loud, happy laughter Jo was accustomed to hear, but soft titters. It wasn't just Jo who hoped to avoid Aunt March's fearful presence.

"Josephine! What is keeping you so long?"

" 'We who are about to die salute you,' " Jo said, and then shouted, "Coming, Aunt March."

"You're fast enough when you think there's a treat coming to you," Aunt March grumbled as Jo made her way to the parlor. "But when it's just a polite request from your great-aunt, you could lose a race to a snail."

"I'm sorry, Aunt March," Jo said. "I was working in the attic."

"On something profitable, I hope," said Aunt March. "And not on another of those silly theatrics of yours."

"Jo's plays are hardly silly, Aunt March," Marmee said. "What is this one called, Jo, dear?"

"*The Curse of Montevideo*," Jo replied.

Aunt March rolled her eyes. "Nothing silly about that," she said.

Jo decided that her next play would be called *The Curse of Concord* and would have a featured role for Aunt March. "Why did you want to see me, Aunt March?" she asked, trying to keep the annoyance out of her voice.

"I should think you would want to see me, Josephine," Aunt March said. "I am your great-aunt, after all, an honored member of your family."

"All my girls love to see you," Marmee said. "But they have so many different interests that keep them busy. You know how it is for girls their age."

"Umph! When I was ten years old, as Jo is now, I was taught to respect my elders," Aunt March declared.

Jo tried to picture Aunt March as a girl her own age, but it was beyond even her wild imagination. Still, perhaps *The Curse of Concord* could feature a beautiful heroine who was turned into an elderly hag. Jo had never tried that plot twist before. In spite of herself, she became excited at the possibilities, and smiled broadly.

"I see I amuse you, Josephine," Aunt March said.

"Yes, Aunt March," Jo said as she thought of Meg acting the part of Aunt March.

Aunt March shook her head.

"I don't think Jo meant that quite the way it sounded," Marmee said. "Jo, sit down. Aunt March has something to ask you."

Jo did as her mother told her. She would do anything for Marmee, who never shouted or demanded or called her Josephine.

"I have what might be called a favor to ask of you, Josephine," Aunt March said.

"A favor?" Jo asked.

"Don't look so startled," Aunt March said. "I've made requests of you in the past."

That was certainly true. But Aunt March never bothered calling them favors. They were simply things Jo was expected to do because Aunt March said so.

"I'm sure Jo will be delighted to help," Marmee said. "Won't you, Jo?"

Jo nodded.

"Not perhaps the politest response, but as good as I can hope for, I suppose," Aunt March said. "Very well. Do you know Mr. and Mrs. Wheeler, Josephine? They live a mile past my house."

"I don't think so," Jo said.

"Your father knows them," Aunt March said. "And your mother has met them as well. They're fine people. Mrs. Wheeler is a Cabot, and Mr. Wheeler's grandmother was an Adams."

That certainly would make them fine people

in Aunt March's mind, Jo thought. Cabots and Adamses were almost as good as royalty in Massachusetts.

"Mr. Wheeler is an abolitionist," Marmee said. "And Mrs. Wheeler and I have worked on committees together to help the poor."

"Then they must be good people," Jo said, smiling at her mother.

"I would have thought my word would suffice," Aunt March said. "But no matter. The Wheelers are my neighbors, and they came to me with a request."

"What do they want, Aunt March?" Jo asked. She couldn't imagine what respectable people could need from a ten-year-old like her.

"Their granddaughter, Pauline, is here on a visit," Aunt March said. "A girl your own age, Josephine. She and her governess will be staying with the Wheelers for much of the winter. Mr. and Mrs. Wheeler's son and daughter-in-law are touring Europe. I gather they do a great deal of traveling."

Jo nodded. She knew children in Concord whose parents went abroad, leaving them in the care of relatives or servants. She couldn't imagine Father and Marmee doing that, even if they'd had the money.

"The Wheelers are concerned that their granddaughter will be lonely," Aunt March continued. "I have mentioned you in the past, and they thought you would be just the right sort of child to keep her entertained."

Jo didn't care to have a stranger shoved at her, but on the other hand, it never hurt to have new actors for her plays. "So is she to come here?" she asked. "Or should I visit her first?"

"You will call first," Aunt March said. "That is the appropriate thing to do. And even if it weren't, you would have to be the one to make the call."

"Why is that, Aunt March?" Jo asked.

"The poor child is blind," Aunt March said, "and as such is deserving of the most basic kind of Christian charity. I'm sure even you, Josephine, can understand that."

CHAPTER 2

Jo never thought of herself as shy. In her household, it was Beth who was frightened of meeting strangers. But there was something about meeting a blind person for the first time, even one Jo's own age, that made her nervous in a way she was totally unaccustomed to.

"How do I look?" she asked Marmee, who was accompanying her on the visit to the Wheelers.

"You look lovely," Marmee said. "The blue of that dress is very becoming, Jo."

Jo had on Meg's best new dress. She'd felt

that none of her own dresses was quite worthy of the occasion.

"I don't know why I'm fussing so," Jo said. "It isn't as though she'll be able to see how I look."

"You're fussing because you care," Marmee said. "And Pauline will sense that from the way you talk and behave. I know I'll be proud of how you conduct yourself, Jo."

Jo hoped, as she always did, that she'd be able to live up to her mother's expectations. Marmee sensed that and gave Jo's hand a reassuring squeeze.

"Oh, my," Jo said as she and Marmee turned off the road. "You'd never find the Wheelers' house unless you knew it was here."

Jo tried to imagine what such privacy felt like. Her home was big enough for her and her parents and her three sisters and Hannah, their housekeeper, but the only private place Jo had was the attic, and her sisters regularly came bounding up there without invitation. To live in a house no one could even see from the road was richness beyond her imagination.

When they finally got to the front door of what Jo immediately labeled a mansion, Marmee knocked. Jo was impressed with how calmly Marmee was behaving.

A butler opened the door. "Mrs. March and Miss Josephine March here to pay a call," Marmee said. "The Wheelers are expecting us."

"I'll take your coats, ma'am," the butler said. "Please wait in here."

Jo and Marmee handed the butler their coats and went into the front parlor. A fire was burning brightly, and they walked to it and warmed themselves.

As they stood in front of the fireplace, an older woman walked in. "Mrs. March," she said, extending her hand to Marmee. "How good of you to come. And this must be Josephine."

"Pleased to meet you, ma'am," Jo said, curtseying as best she could. Meg did much better at that than she did, Jo thought. It was unfair that Pauline should be Jo's age and not Meg's.

"I'm delighted that a girl my granddaughter's age has agreed to pay her a call," Mrs. Wheeler said. "It is very good of you, Josephine, to give up an afternoon this way."

"I'm sure Jo will have as good a time as Pauline," Marmee said.

Mrs. Wheeler sighed. "Pauline is not an easy child," she said. "Of course, since she was born with such a terrible curse, we can hardly expect her to behave as a normal girl would. But my son and daughter-in-law have done all they can for her, I'm sure. Pauline will never lack for anything."

"And there is nothing that can be done about her sight?" Marmee asked.

"She's been taken to the best doctors in Boston and New York," Mrs. Wheeler replied. "When they offered no hope, my son even took her to London for an examination. All the doctors agree she will be sightless until the day she dies. We can but pray that in Heaven the gift of sight will be hers."

"That poor child," Marmee said. "I'm sure, though, that a visit with Jo will provide her with entertainment, even if it's just for one afternoon."

"Pauline is expecting you, Josephine," Mrs. Wheeler said. "Her room is upstairs, the third door on the right. And I thank you again for visiting. Pauline's life has so little to cheer her. I know how she's been looking forward to this visit."

"I'll try to do my best," Jo said.

"I'll come for you in a little while," Marmee said.

Jo left the parlor and walked up the stairs. She felt exactly the way Count Rudolph had felt in her last play, *The Lost Treasure of the Bourbons*, when he was on his way to his beheading.

She counted the doors and knocked on the third one. "Come in," a woman's voice said, and Jo turned the knob.

"You must be Josephine," the woman said, ushering Jo into the room. It was a lovely bedroom, far grander than the one Jo shared with Meg. There was a fire burning merrily. Jo couldn't imagine greater luxury than having a fireplace in one's bedroom. She and Meg woke up on cold winter mornings and raced to get dressed so that they could warm up in the kitchen by the woodstove.

"I'm Miss Johnson," the woman said, "Pauline's governess. Pauline, Josephine March is here to call on you."

Jo looked around the room and saw a girl sitting quietly in a chair by the fireplace. "Everyone calls me Jo," Jo said. "Should I go over and sit by her side?"

"That would be lovely," Miss Johnson said. "Wouldn't it, Pauline?" Pauline remained quiet. "She's shy," Miss Johnson whispered.

"I can hear you," Pauline said. "I'm blind, not deaf."

"Yes, we know, dear," Miss Johnson said. "Very well, girls. I'll leave you alone for your visit." She smiled at Jo and left the room before Jo could come up with a convincing argument for her to stay.

Jo crossed the room and sat in a chair opposite Pauline's. Pauline was a pretty girl with blond hair. Nothing about her announced her blindness.

"Hello," Jo said. "I'm Jo. My aunt March knows your grandparents."

"I know," Pauline said. "They told me you were coming. They said you must be a very good girl to pay me a visit."

"I'm not," Jo said. "Good, I mean. My sister Meg is, and my sister Beth. Meg's good because it's important to her and she works at it, and Bethy's just so sweet, she has to be good. But I'm not. I don't think my sister Amy is good either, but she gets away with things. She's the youngest, you know, and she's pretty. She has blond hair, just the same as you, only hers is curlier." Jo realized she would give anything to have any one of her sisters by her side just then, so that she wouldn't be alone with this strange, silent girl. "Have you any sisters?" she asked.

"Yes," Pauline said. "Sisters and brothers."

"Where are they?" Jo asked. "I mean, are they visiting your grandparents also?"

"My sisters are in Europe with my parents,"

Pauline said. "My brothers are in school. I can't go to school, and naturally my parents don't want me with them while they travel. And that's why I'm staying here."

"Why is that natural?" Jo asked. "If your sisters can go with your parents, why can't you?"

"Because they can see," Pauline replied. "My parents are hoping to make brilliant matches for my sisters, and it will do them no good to have a blind girl along."

"Well, you've been to Europe already," Jo said. "Your grandmother said you've been to London."

"I was two," Pauline said. "I have no memories of the trip."

"No, of course not," Jo said. "Where do you live when you're not visiting Concord?"

"Boston," Pauline said. "But it doesn't matter where, really. I could live on the moon or in Paris just as well. I never leave the house. I rarely leave my bedroom. I have a governess. This year it's Miss Johnson. And a maid takes

16

care of all my needs. They see to it that I'm bathed and dressed and fed."

"But you must do more than that," Jo said. "Whom do you play with?"

"I don't play with others," Pauline said. "How can I, when I can't see what they're doing?"

"And you don't go to school?" Jo asked.

"School is for those who can see," Pauline answered. "My governess teaches me all I'll need to know. She reads to me and tells me stories about history. She teaches me songs. I have a very good memory. She recites poems to me until I can recite them myself. My father likes that. When he asks for me, I go to the parlor and recite a new poem and he says there's nothing wrong with my brain at least, and that makes him feel much better. Would you like me to recite something for you?"

"Very much," Jo said, and as Pauline began her recitation of "The Village Blacksmith," she thought about Pauline's sad, lonely life and how much she wished she didn't have to be part of it.

CHAPTER 3

"And that was all you did?" Meg asked as she, Beth, and Amy gathered around Jo to hear how the visit had gone. "You sat there and listened as Pauline recited poetry?"

"There was nothing else to do," Jo said. "I offered to read to her, but she said Miss Johnson spent hours every day doing that and she hardly needed me to do the same."

"She sounds terrible," Amy said. "But we should take pity on her. How awful it must be to have blond hair and not be able to see it."

"That's not all she can't see," Beth said.

19

"She can't see sunsets or daisies or kittens. Or the love on her parents' faces."

"I'm not sure there is any love there," Jo said. "They're ashamed of her for being blind."

"It's not her fault she's blind," Amy said. "No one would choose not to be able to see her own hair."

"Especially if it's blond," Meg said. "Honestly, Amy, not knowing you have blond hair isn't the worst thing about being blind."

" 'Blind' and 'blond,' " Amy said. "They're practically the same word. You don't think all girls with blond hair might end up blind, do you?"

"I don't even think all blind girls will end up blond," Meg said. "Don't be such a goose, Amy."

"I feel sorry for Pauline," Beth said. "All alone in her darkness."

"She's never alone," Jo said. "She has a governess and a maid. She told me she's never alone for a single moment, for fear she'll hurt herself."

"She's alone anyway," Beth said. "Sometimes when we have company and I feel frightened, it doesn't matter that you or Marmee or Father is here. Inside me, I'm totally alone. I think it must be that way for Pauline."

"I'd feel sorry for Jo, except that I think she's feeling sorry enough for herself," Meg said.

"You'd feel sorry for yourself too if you'd been forced to say you'd pay another call tomorrow," Jo said. "I was so sure I'd have *The Curse of Montevideo* ready for its first rehearsal in a few days. And now I'm not even certain it'll be finished by next week. It gets dark so awfully early now, and the attic gets so cold, it's harder and harder to work there."

"You will finish the play soon, won't you, Jo?" Amy asked. "You said it has my first really big part."

"And a great one it is," Jo said. "But I don't know when I'll be able to finish it now. It might even have to wait until springtime."

"I don't know if I can wait that long," Amy said. "Work in our room, Jo. I'll keep quiet, and Beth never makes any noise."

"I'd welcome noise," Jo said. "Are you sure none of you wants to visit Pauline with me tomorrow? At least then we can talk to each other while she listens."

"I'd go with you, Jo," Beth said. "But it frightens me so to think of all those other people there. Her grandparents and her governess and all the servants."

"And I'd go with you, but I already promised Mary Howe I'd call on her," Meg said, not looking the least bit sad that she'd made such arrangements.

"I should dearly love to go," Amy said. "But I have a cold, and Marmee would never allow me to walk such a long distance when I'm already so ill." She sniffed dramatically to prove her point.

"Then I suppose I must go by myself," Jo said. "Although I don't know how I'll endure another such afternoon."

"Pauline endures them every day of her life," Beth said. "You can spare one more for her, can't you, Jo?"

Jo shook her head. "It's confounded hard to be good," she said.

"Don't use slang," Meg said. "And yes, Jo, it is confounded hard."

Now that Jo knew the way to the Wheelers' house, there was no need for Marmee to go with her. The day was colder than the previous one, and Jo had to admit that it was no weather for Amy to be walking about in. Jo no longer had Meg's good dress to wear, since Meg had it on herself, but Jo didn't care nearly so much what she looked like. She couldn't believe that she'd agreed to visit a second day in a row. It wasn't as though Pauline had had a good time either.

But Mrs. Wheeler had acted as though Jo would be returning the very next day, and somehow Marmee had conveyed to Jo that she had to accept.

This time it was Jo who knocked on the door and announced herself to the butler. Mrs. Wheeler was waiting for her in the parlor.

"It is so kind of you to return so soon," Mrs. Wheeler told Jo. "Miss Johnson says Pauline is quite pleased about it."

"Didn't you ask Pauline yourself?" Jo asked. She was sure that was a rude question, but she no longer cared.

"Of course I did," Mrs. Wheeler said. "After you left, I went to Pauline's room to see how she was feeling. But she simply said she was weary from your visit, and I left her to recover. And then this morning I was in church, and I've scarcely had time to speak with her today."

Jo knew her parents would always find time to speak with her. Even Aunt March found the time, whether Jo wanted her to or not. "I'll go upstairs now," she said. "I'm sure Pauline is waiting."

"Thank you, Josephine," Mrs. Wheeler said.

Jo went directly to Pauline's room. Miss

Johnson was sitting opposite Pauline, reading to her from the Bible. Jo waited until she had finished the chapter and then announced herself.

"I'll leave you girls alone for your visit," Miss Johnson said. "Josephine, please try not to overtire Pauline, as you did yesterday."

"I'll do my best," Jo said, although she couldn't imagine how she could have overtired anyone by simply sitting and keeping quiet. "Did I really overtire you?" she asked Pauline once the governess had left the room.

"I tire easily," Pauline said.

"But why?" Jo asked. "You're not an invalid, are you?"

"I'm blind, aren't I?" Pauline retorted.

"Do blind people get tired more easily?" Jo asked.

"I don't know about other blind people," Pauline said. "I'm not allowed to have any dealings with other blind people."

"Why not?" Jo asked. There was such a lot about blindness she knew nothing of.

"Most blind people are poor," Pauline said.

"They beg on the streets. I will never have to beg on the streets."

"That's good, I suppose," Jo said, although part of her thought it would be more interesting to beg on the streets than to sit around doing nothing in the same room every day.

"I am very fortunate," Pauline said. "Everyone tells me so. I'm well taken care of. You don't have a governess, do you, or a maid to take care of all your needs?"

"No," Jo said.

"Are you poor?" Pauline asked.

"Aunt March says we're poor," replied Jo. "But we don't beg on the streets."

"Miss Johnson said you appeared quite respectable," Pauline declared.

"I look less respectable today," Jo said. "Yesterday I wore my sister Meg's dress, and today I'm wearing one of my own. I wear all Meg's old clothes, and they're fine when they get to me, but I always manage to get them dirty somehow."

"All my clothes are new," Pauline said. "My mother's seamstress makes them for me."

"They're very pretty," Jo said. "You look quite nice."

"It doesn't matter," Pauline said. "I could wear rags, except that it would shame my parents. No one sees me. And, of course, I can't see myself."

"I know you tire easily and all that," Jo said. "But I still don't understand why you have to stay in your room all the time."

"Because it's so hard for me to get around," Pauline said. "And no one would want to play with me anyway."

"We would," Jo said. "My sisters and I. They would have come with me today if they could." Then she had a thought. She wasn't sure whether it was a good one or a wicked one. "You must visit us," she said. "Next Saturday. You can even spend the night at our house. It's always a treat to have a guest stay over."

"I don't know if my grandparents will let me," Pauline said.

"I'm sure they will," Jo said. "We're perfectly respectable. Say yes, Pauline, and I'm

27

sure you'll have a fine time playing with my sisters and me."

Pauline sat absolutely still. "Very well," she said at last. "If my grandmother consents, I'll pay you a call."

Jo smiled. Anything had to be better than another endless afternoon spent sitting quietly in Pauline's bedroom.

CHAPTER 4

"There you are, Jo," said Willie Howe after school on Thursday. "Freddie and James and I are going to go skating on Walden Pond Saturday afternoon. We're going to see who can race across the fastest. Do you want to join us?"

"I'd love to," Jo replied. She had beaten all the boys in races over the summer but had never been challenged in a skating competition.

"Good," Willie said. "Freddie was sure he could beat you, but James and I both think you'll race faster than he can. Of course, I'm the fastest and will beat all of you."

"Don't be so sure of that," Jo said, but she laughed. It was a beautiful winter day, crisp and clear. It would be dark very soon, now that the school day had ended, but the sun was bright enough to give them a feeling of warmth.

"What are you laughing about?" Meg asked, walking up to them accompanied by Mary Howe, her best friend and Willie's sister.

"Willie's challenged me to a skating race," Jo replied. "Across Walden Pond on Saturday afternoon."

"What fun," Mary said. "Meg, you and I must go and watch the race. You can cheer Jo on, and I'll root for Willie."

"Jo can't race," Meg said.

"And why not?" Jo demanded. "I'm at least as good a skater as Freddie."

"What does Freddie have to do with this?" Meg said. "Not that it matters. You can't race that day because Pauline is coming to visit."

"Oh, no," Jo said. "I forgot."

"Who's Pauline?" Willie said.

"She's Mr. and Mrs. Wheeler's grand-daughter," Meg said. "And Jo invited her to visit us on Saturday. She's staying overnight."

"Then bring her along," Willie said. "She can race too, if she'd like. I can beat her also." He grinned at the thought.

"Pauline doesn't skate," Jo said. "She's blind."

"I've heard about her," Mary said. "My father said her blindness is a terrible punishment from God. I didn't realize you knew her, Jo."

"Aunt March has forced her upon me," Jo said.

"Could you bring her to the pond anyway?" Willie asked. "Mary and Meg could keep her company while we raced."

"And then everyone could come back to our house for hot chocolate," Mary said. "Beth and Amy could come too. It would be so much fun."

"What do you think, Jo?" Meg asked.

Jo couldn't imagine anything more fun than racing against Willie, Freddie, and James, followed by hot chocolate at the Howes' house. "I'd love to," she said, but then she thought about Pauline. "But somehow I can't see Pauline wanting to."

"Because she's blind?" Mary asked. "She can taste, can't she? She'd enjoy the chocolate and the company."

"She's very quiet," Jo said, not knowing how else to describe Pauline.

"Even quieter than Beth?" Mary asked.

"Not in the same way as Beth," said Jo. "I don't think she'd have a good time at all. She wouldn't be able to see us race, and I doubt she's ever skated herself. I don't see how I could ask her to join us."

"Perhaps you could change the date of her visit," Mary suggested. "She could call on you the weekend after this one instead."

"She is visiting her grandparents for the winter," Meg said. "Isn't she, Jo? She'd have plenty of chances to call on us."

Jo thought about Pauline, whose life consisted of sitting in her bedroom, being read to, and memorizing poetry. If Jo had had to live like that, she'd have died of boredom before the first crocus bloomed. "Pauline doesn't have much fun in life," she said. "She's probably been looking forward to her visit all week. I can't disappoint her."

"Then we'll have to race without you," Willie said. "Bother. I was looking forward to seeing you beat Freddie. And to beating you myself, of course."

"Some other time," Jo said. "Come, Meg. We'd best be getting home."

"That was very good of you," Meg said to Jo as they walked off. "I know you must be disappointed."

"That *was* good of me," Jo said, and she felt pleased both at her own nobility and at Meg's noticing it. In fact, she was so pleased with herself, she didn't even mind when Meg laughed at her lack of modesty.

"This is an excellent soup," Father said that night at supper. "Hannah has outdone herself."

"There is something so comforting about hot

33

LIBRARY
DEXTER SCHOOLS
DEXTER, NM 88230

soup on a cold winter's night," Marmee said. "Jo, dearest, you've hardly touched yours."

"I've been thinking," Jo said.

"I never knew that to keep you from eating," Amy said, and her sisters laughed. Jo was known for her healthy appetite.

"What were you thinking about, Jo?" her father asked.

"About Pauline's blindness," Jo replied.

"Mary and Willie Howe invited all of us to watch Willie race Jo on Walden Pond," Meg said. "And then we were to go to their house for hot chocolate. But Jo turned down the invitation because of Pauline."

"That wasn't what I was thinking about," Jo said. "I was wondering why Pauline is blind."

"Some damage to her nervous system, I suppose," Father said. "She was born blind, I believe."

"But why was she born blind?" Jo asked. "Why her and not me? Was God punishing her for something?"

"God does not punish babies," Father declared.

"Then was He punishing her parents?" Jo asked. "I've heard people say things like that, the sins of the father being visited upon the children."

"Is that what you think, Jo?" her father asked.

"I don't know," she said. "I don't think so. It doesn't seem very fair."

"But the world isn't fair," Meg said. "If it were, there wouldn't be slavery."

"And women would have the vote," said Beth.

"And we'd have lots of money," said Amy.

The others turned to her.

"All right," Amy said. "*Everyone* would have lots of money. But we'd deserve it because we're so good. Isn't that right, Father?"

"Goodness and money have never gone hand in glove," said Father. "But Meg is right. There are many injustices in this world, and we must fight to right them."

"So Pauline is blind because of an injustice?" Jo persisted.

"I'm sure it seems that way to her," Father said. "Just as Amy sees it as an injustice that she isn't rich. Although blindness is a far greater cause for suffering than not having enough money for pretty new clothes."

"I suppose," said Amy. "Although I can't see why I can't have pretty clothes when Pauline, who's blind, has beautiful ones."

"Do you think God loves Pauline more because she's blind?" Beth asked. "I know I love my damaged dollies more than the healthy ones."

"God loves all of us equally," Father said. "Although I suspect He has a special place in His heart for you, Beth."

"But you still haven't answered me, Father," Jo said. "Why was Pauline chosen for blindness?"

"We can't know God's purpose," Father said, "any more than we can guess the future. Perhaps Pauline will do something great in her life because she is blind. How can we know that now?"

"Perhaps her suffering will make you more compassionate, Jo," said Marmee. "Who knows? Years from now, you might show a small kindness to someone because of your friendship with Pauline."

Jo knew she couldn't call what she had with Pauline a friendship. Still, it was good to know there might be a reason why Pauline was blind and that maybe the reason wasn't a bad one.

CHAPTER 5

"She's here!" Amy cried, after spending nearly an hour staring out the window. "That must be her carriage. Oh, Jo, it's even finer than Aunt March's. They must be so rich. How do I look?"

"It doesn't matter how you look," Meg said. "What matters is how you behave."

"I'll be good," Amy vowed. "Oh, Beth, isn't this exciting? I've never met a blind girl before. And such a rich one!"

"If you say another such foolish thing, I swear, Amy March, I'll box your ears," Jo declared. "Now, keep quiet."

"If I'm quiet, she won't know I'm here," Amy said.

"That's just the sort of comment I don't want to hear," Jo said.

"Don't worry, Jo," Meg said. "I'll see to it that Amy behaves."

"I'll be good too," Beth said.

"Good," Jo said. "You talk more, and Amy, you talk less, and we'll all make it through this visit."

The girls were still laughing as Pauline entered the house. Jo noticed that Miss Johnson walked a step ahead of Pauline. Pauline had hold of Miss Johnson's upper arm, and Miss Johnson spoke to her quietly, telling her how many steps there were and where the door was.

"We're here," Miss Johnson said. "With nary a mishap."

"Welcome, Pauline. Hello, Miss Johnson," Marmee said, coming to the front door. "My, it's turned cold. Come into the parlor and get warm."

"I'll lead you, Pauline," Miss Johnson said, doing just that. She helped Pauline off with her coat and got her seated. "I'll be going now," the governess then said. "Pauline will have little need of me on such an exciting visit."

"No," Pauline said. "Please stay, Miss Johnson."

"You know I've made arrangements to visit my sister," Miss Johnson said. She added to Marmee, "I rarely have a chance to see her, Pauline so needs my services. Now, Pauline, I'll be back with the carriage tomorrow after breakfast. And be sure to thank Mrs. March for her kindness in letting you stay overnight with her daughters."

"It's no kindness at all," Marmee said. "My girls have spoken of nothing else all week. Girls, why don't you take Pauline to Jo's room, and take her things there with you?"

"Miss Johnson, please don't leave me," Pauline said.

"Now, Pauline, behave yourself," Miss Johnson said. "You'll be safely home tomorrow." She turned to Marmee. "She hates to leave the familiar," she said. "But I'm sure she'll be little bother once she settles down."

"Come, Pauline," Jo said. "It's me, Jo."

"I recognize your voice," Pauline said.

Jo put her arm out, the way Miss Johnson had, and waited for Pauline to rest her hand on it. But then she realized that Pauline couldn't see what she had done. She took Pauline's hand and placed it on her upper arm. "Follow me," she said.

Pauline rose from the chair. She clutched Jo's arm with her right hand and swung her left arm around as though searching for objects in the air.

"Don't swing so," Jo said. "You'll knock something over."

"Jo," Marmee said.

"She will," Jo said. The parlor was crowded even when it wasn't filled with people. Sure enough, after just a few steps, Pauline had knocked over a pile of books that Father had left on the edge of a shelf.

"Why don't you hold my hand also?" Beth

suggested. "I'm Beth, Jo's sister. I'll help you get upstairs."

"I can help too," Amy said. "There's a door over there, Pauline, and then you're in the hallway."

"Pauline won't know what 'over there' is," Meg said. "Pauline, I'm Meg. Don't worry. You'll feel at home here in no time."

"Miss Johnson," Pauline pleaded, but Miss Johnson was already halfway out the door. Jo wished she could go with her.

"There are lots of steps," Amy said. "But I bet there are more steps where you live, aren't there, Pauline?"

"Jo?" Pauline said. "Don't let me go."

"I won't," Jo said, stifling a sigh. Somehow she hadn't thought about what it would be like to move with Pauline around the house. She realized that was because she'd never seen Pauline move. She always sat so still. "We'll go to my room and you'll sit down and then you can stay there until tomorrow morning if you like," she said. "We can bring your food to you, just the way you have it at home."

"Marmee won't like that," Amy said. "She and Father were looking forward to having Pauline eat with us. They said so just this morning."

"How many more steps are there?" Pauline asked. "The steps are so steep, they scare me. How will I get down them?"

"We'll help you down," Meg said. "There are only four more, and then you'll be upstairs. And our bedroom is just a few feet away. You're practically there already."

Jo led Pauline into her bedroom. "Here we are," she said. "Amy, do you have Pauline's bag?"

"Of course I do," Amy said. "What's the matter? Can't you see?"

The other girls fell absolutely silent. "Oh," Amy said. "That was a terrible thing for me to say. I'm sorry, Pauline."

Pauline had let go of Beth's hand and was swinging her left arm wildly again. "I want to sit down," she said. "Where can I sit?"

"There's a chair right here," Jo said, trying to lead Pauline to it. But as she swung her arm about, Pauline knocked over more books and a basket of yarn.

"Don't worry," Meg said. "I'll pick everything up."

"This chair isn't very comfortable," Pauline said, sinking into it at last. "Isn't there a more comfortable one?"

"Not in this room," Meg said. "We only have the one chair here."

"There are more comfortable chairs in the parlor," Beth said. "Would you like to go back there?"

"No," Pauline said. "No. I have to rest for a while."

"Would you like to lie down?" Meg asked. "There's a bed just a few inches away from you."

"I'll just sit still," Pauline said.

"Jo said you like to sing," Beth said. "We sing a lot. Perhaps there's some song we could all sing."

"And Jo said you like to be read to," Amy said. "Maybe Jo could read to us from her newest play, *The Curse of Montevideo.*

44

Jo says there's a perfectly splendid part in it for me."

"And Jo says you recite poetry beautifully," Meg said. "Perhaps you'd honor us with one of your recitations."

"Was I invited here to entertain you?" Pauline asked. "Do you want to see the blind girl perform her tricks?"

The girls fell silent.

"Jo, are you still there?" Pauline asked.

"Yes, I am," Jo said.

"Don't leave me," Pauline said. "Your sisters can go, if they want, but you must stay with me. Do you understand? You simply must stay."

"I'm not going anywhere," Jo said. "But don't you want to do something besides just sit?"

"Would you like to meet my dollies?" Beth asked. "I'm sure they'd enjoy meeting you."

"Or you could hear Jo's play," Amy suggested again. "You wouldn't be entertaining us that way. Jo would be entertaining you. And I do so want to hear my part."

"The play's in the attic," Jo said. "I could get it and be back here in no time."

"No," Pauline said. "You promised you wouldn't leave."

"I could get it," Meg said.

"No," Jo said. She hated to have anyone go through her papers. "I'll get it later, when Pauline lets me."

"Then what are we to do?" Amy asked. "Just sit here until suppertime?"

"If that's what Pauline wants," Jo said. She scowled, and only the knowledge that Pauline couldn't see the face she was making gave her any pleasure.

*I*f it had been misery for Jo to sit quietly
by Pauline's side in the Wheelers' house,
it was even worse for her to do so in her
own bedroom.

It was no help to Jo that her sisters were
there. Meg picked up the yarn basket and began to knit. Beth left the room and returned
with her dolls. When Pauline expressed no in-
terest in getting to know them, Beth contented
herself with silent play. Amy found her
sketchpad and began drawing Pauline.

"You're a wonderful model," she said to
Pauline. "Sitting so quietly. Even Beth moves

around too much when I try to draw her, and Jo never seems to sit still."

"I'm sitting still now," Jo said. She had a cramp in her leg, but every time she tried to shift her weight, Pauline grabbed her arm and held her in place.

After almost two hours, Jo thought she couldn't stand any more. "I think I'll go to the attic now and get my play," she said.

"Oh, yes, do," Amy said.

"No," Pauline said. "You promised you wouldn't leave my side, Jo."

Meg put down her knitting needles. "I think I hear Marmee calling me," she said. "Will you excuse me, Pauline?"

"I hear her too," Amy said. "Wait for me, Meg. I'll go with you."

Jo wasn't at all sure Marmee had called for anyone, but she couldn't blame her sisters for wanting to escape.

"If you'd go downstairs, I could play the piano for you," Beth suggested. "And we could all sing. Jo says you have a wonderful memory, Pauline. Maybe we could teach you some songs you don't already know."

"What a good idea," Jo said. "Wouldn't you enjoy that, Pauline?"

"You won't leave me?" Pauline said. "You'll stay by my side, Jo?"

"If that's what you want," Jo said.

"Very well," Pauline said. "Help me up, Jo."

Jo got up slowly, her cramped leg tingling, and then helped Pauline rise from the chair.

"I'll go down first," Beth said, "and ask Meg and Amy to join us. Meg has a beautiful singing voice, Pauline. I know you'll enjoy singing with her."

"I've never sung with anyone before," Pauline said.

"Not even with your sisters?" Beth asked.

"They're much older than I am," Pauline said. "And they don't like to spend time with me."

"You'll like singing with us," Beth said. "I'll meet you downstairs by the piano."

Jo led Pauline out of the bedroom. Pauline began swinging her left arm again, but Jo didn't stop to pick things up.

"You won't let go of me?" Pauline said as they reached the staircase. "The stairs are so steep, Jo. They frighten me."

"Just hold on to my arm," Jo said. The stairs *were* steep, and Jo was unaccustomed to having someone grasping at her. "I don't think this is going to work," she said to Pauline. "Why don't I get a step ahead of you, and you can hold on to my shoulders as we go down."

"I don't know how to do it that way," Pauline said.

"It will be fine," Jo said. She edged her way in front of Pauline and began walking down the stairs.

"Jo, where are you?" Pauline cried.

"I'm just ahead of you," Jo said. "Hold my shoulders, Pauline."

But Pauline began swinging both her arms instead. She hit Jo on the side of the head, and Jo stumbled and nearly lost her balance.

"Jo! Jo!" Pauline cried.

But Jo was too busy trying to right herself to pay attention to Pauline.

"Jo, I'm going to fall," Pauline said, and then, as though to prove her point, she began to stumble down the steps.

Jo tried to catch her, but her leg, which was still numb, gave way. Pauline tumbled on top of her, and the two girls rolled down the stairs, reaching the bottom at almost the same time.

"Girls, are you all right?" Meg asked as she ran to the foot of the staircase.

"I'm fine, I think," Jo said, trying to stand up. But Pauline stayed motionless on the floor.

"Pauline, are you all right?" Meg asked.

Pauline began to cry. "I want to go home," she said. "I won't stay here a minute longer."

"You can't go now," Meg said. "It's dark already, and your carriage won't be here to pick you up until tomorrow."

"I don't care," Pauline said. "I'm going home now. Jo, take me home."

"You can't, Pauline," Meg said. "Marmee and Father had to go out a few minutes ago. Wait until they get back."

"I won't wait, I won't!" Pauline screamed. "I'm going right now, even if I have to go by myself."

"Jo, what do you think?" Meg asked. Beth and Amy stood there quietly, waiting for Jo to speak.

"We'll be fine," Jo said. "Amy, get our coats. Beth, ask Hannah for a lantern."

"I don't like the idea of your walking back here alone at night," Meg said.

"Then I'll spend the night at Aunt March's," Jo said. "I'll be back tomorrow in time for church."

"Marmee won't like it," Amy said as she went to get the coats.

Jo knew that Amy was right. But she could feel Pauline trembling at her side and knew just as well that it would be a mistake to force Pauline to stay there a minute longer.

CHAPTER 7

*I*t had been a long walk to the Wheelers' house when Jo had gone there with Marmee and on her own. It was going to be an even longer walk with Pauline by her side.

"Don't walk too fast," Pauline said as they began the journey. "I don't want to fall again."

"You won't," Jo said, uncomfortably aware that she'd promised that before and Pauline had tumbled down the stairs anyway. "I'll be careful."

But it was hard to walk with Pauline holding on to her right arm, and the lantern in her left hand. Jo was glad of the lantern, since it was dark; even though she knew the route to Aunt March's well, it was comforting to have some illumination. The farther they walked away from Jo's home, the fewer houses there were and the darker the road became.

"You're walking too fast," Pauline cried. "Slow down, Jo."

"I'm sorry," Jo said. "This is hard."

"It's harder for me," Pauline said bitterly.

Jo stopped for a moment, and Pauline was forced to stop as well. "It *is* harder for you, isn't it?" Jo said.

Pauline laughed. It was the first time Jo had heard her laugh. "You've just realized that?" Pauline asked.

Jo had been so busy feeling sorry for herself, she hadn't bothered thinking about what it must be like for Pauline. "I'm sorry," she said. "I'll try to do better."

"I'll try too," Pauline said. "It's just that I'm used to Miss Johnson and the way she walks. Is it much farther to my grandparents'?"

"I'm afraid so," Jo replied. "We're nowhere near Aunt March's yet, and it's a full mile after that to your grandparents'."

"I've never walked so far," Pauline said.

"You've never done much of anything, have you?" Jo inquired.

"Not really," Pauline said. "Except go to London when I was two."

"I've always dreamed of going to Europe," Jo said. "The way your sisters are doing. Not to make great matches, but to see all the sights."

"I'll never do either," Pauline said. "No one will want to marry a blind girl."

"Why not?" Jo asked, but before Pauline had a chance to respond, a fierce gust of wind suddenly blew, nearly knocking her over. Even worse, the wind blew out the flame in the lantern.

"Oh, no," Jo said.

"What?" Pauline asked, and Jo could hear the terror in her voice. "What is it, Jo? Are you all right?"

"I'm fine," Jo said. "But the lantern's gone out."

"Is there any light at all?" Pauline asked.

"Not much," Jo said. "The sky's suddenly full of luminous clouds, which is strange. I'm not sure what it means."

"We'll be all right if we stay on the road, won't we, Jo?" Pauline asked. "It's a straight path, isn't it?"

"No," Jo said. "There are turns to Aunt March's, and then more to your grandparents'."

"What should we do?" Pauline asked.

"I don't know," Jo said. "I can't see any houses to go to." The wind began howling then, and in a moment snow began to fall. The snow was heavy and wet.

"What's happening?" Pauline asked. "Jo, are you still here?"

"Yes, I am," Jo said. "I'm sorry. I was just bending over, trying to find the lantern."

"Why?" Pauline asked. "Will it do us any good?"

"No," Jo said, not caring to explain that the March family couldn't afford to lose their possessions by the side of the road.

"Take hold of me," Pauline said. "Jo, is that snow falling?"

"Yes, it is," Jo said. "And I can't believe how fast it's coming down."

"Jo, I'm cold," Pauline said. "Don't leave me here alone."

"I would never do that," Jo said. "Here I am." She took Pauline's hand and held it in hers. "We might as well walk hand in hand," she said. "I can't see much better than you."

"Then I should lead," Pauline said. "At least I have experience being blind."

"We'll get through this together," Jo said. "All we have to do is find a house and stay there until the storm passes." But the snow was falling so fiercely, Jo couldn't see anything on either side of the road.

"Do you know where we are?" Pauline asked.

"No," Jo said. "I think we should make a

turn soon to get to Aunt March's, but it's hard to tell where the road is. I've never seen it snow this hard before."

"The wind frightens me more," Pauline said. "It cuts into my bones."

"I think we should turn here," Jo said, trying to sound confident. "Hold on, Pauline."

But as soon as they had made the turn, Jo realized it was a mistake. It might have been the right direction to go in, but the wind was blowing right at them and every step they took was a struggle.

"I'm sorry," Pauline said. "This is all my fault. Can you ever forgive me, Jo?"

"It's my fault too," Jo said. "I shouldn't have invited you to my house without having thought about it. I never think first. I always just do."

"The way I did," Pauline said. "Insisting on going home on foot instead of waiting for the carriage tomorrow."

"The way it's snowing, you might have been stranded at my house for days," Jo said.

"I would have liked that," Pauline said. "It's new things that frighten me. Once I know where things are in a place, I like being there."

"Is that why you stay in your room all the time?" Jo asked. "Because you know where things are there?"

But Pauline didn't have a chance to respond. "Oh, no!" Jo cried.

"What is it?" Pauline asked. "What's the matter?"

"We're not on the road anymore," Jo said. "I just bumped into a tree."

Pauline swung her free arm around. "There are trees all around us," she said. "Do you think we've been off the road for a long time, Jo?"

"I don't know," Jo said. "I'm not sure of anything anymore."

"Do people die in snowstorms?" Pauline asked.

"I suppose so," Jo said. "But we're not going to. We're too close to houses. We're bound to find one."

"I can't hear you!" Pauline cried. "Jo, the wind is getting stronger. I can't hear you anymore."

"I'm still here!" Jo shouted. "Whatever you do, don't lose hold of me."

Pauline squeezed Jo's hand. "We have to find shelter," she screamed. "Jo, can you get us back on the road?"

"I'll try!" Jo shouted back. "Hold on!"

Jo used her free right arm the way Pauline had, swinging it around, trying to find open spaces. There were trees all around, and bushes, and the girls kept bumping into things and stumbling in their attempt to make their way through.

Jo tried to picture just where it was they could be, but the more they walked, the more disoriented she became. For all she knew, they were a minute from Aunt March's. Or they could be miles away, lost in the forest, with death a real possibility.

The snow was falling harder still. Jo could no longer see more than a foot or two ahead. The wind attacked her savagely. Only Pauline's presence by her side kept her from crying out in terror.

"The wind's stronger!" Pauline screamed.

"I know," Jo shouted back. "I think that's a good sign."

Pauline began to laugh. It was a hysterical laugh, and it took all Jo's strength not to give in to it.

"I mean it," Jo shouted. "I think it means we've found a clearing."

"I think you're right!" Pauline yelled. "I'm not feeling any more trees. Will there be a house nearby?"

"There should be," Jo said, although she wasn't at all sure that they could find a house. There were meadows in the area, vast empty spaces used for grazing cows and growing corn and wheat. It would be all too easy to lose their way in a field and walk in circles until they collapsed from exhaustion.

"We have to keep moving!" Pauline shouted. "No matter how hard it is, Jo, we have to stay on our feet!"

The girls huddled together as they walked through the open space. Jo's eyes filled with tears from the wind, and the heavy snow made it even harder to walk.

"Straight line, Jo," Pauline said. "We have to walk straight, or else we'll get even more lost."

"Straight to a house!" Jo cried, hoping that would prove true. She had no idea whether they were walking straight, or even whether straight was the best way for them to go. But she knew as well as Pauline that walking in a circle could lead them to their deaths.

"Something's different!" Pauline shouted. "There's a difference in the wind, Jo."

It took Jo a moment to feel the difference, but then she sensed what Pauline had noticed. "There's something up ahead," Jo said. "Maybe it's a building."

"Can you see any lights?" Pauline asked.

"No," Jo said. "But any kind of shelter is better than none. Stay with me, Pauline. I think we're almost there."

CHAPTER 8

Jo's free arm touched the side of a building. "It's here, all right," she said to Pauline. "Can you feel it?"

"Yes," Pauline said. "Oh, yes, Jo. Let's find the door and get inside."

It took a few minutes of fighting the wind and the snow before Jo could locate the door. She didn't even bother to knock, but tried opening it instead. Much to her relief, the door swung open.

The girls ran inside, and Jo pushed the door shut. It wasn't much warmer inside than it had been out, but the wind didn't cut into them so much, and there was no snow falling on them.

"Is it a house?" Pauline asked. "Can you see what kind of place this is, Jo?"

"I'm not sure yet," Jo said. "It's even darker in here than it was outside. Keep holding on to me, Pauline, until we can figure out where we are."

But it was Pauline who discovered it first. "It's a carriage house," she said. "I can feel the carriage right in front of us."

Jo reached out and felt the carriage as well. "A carriage house means there must be a real house nearby," she said.

"We don't dare try to find it now," Pauline said. "We could get lost all over again. Besides, there's probably a blanket or a fur throw in the carriage that we can wrap ourselves up in. We need the warmth, Jo, or else we might freeze to death."

"You're right," Jo said. "Let me climb in and see what I can find." She bumped herself a few more times but managed to scramble into the carriage. "There is a fur throw!" she called to Pauline. "Do you think you can get up here yourself?"

"If you can, I can," Pauline said. Jo counted two bumps before Pauline joined her inside the carriage.

The girls snuggled together under the fur wrap. "I'm taking my shoes and stockings off," Pauline said. "My feet are so wet, I think they'll get warm faster if I do."

"That's a good idea," Jo said. "I've never been this cold in my life."

"I'm cold like this all the time," Pauline said. "Shivering and shaking."

"Even in the summer?" Jo asked.

"Sometimes even then," Pauline said. "When I'm afraid, the way I was today, I start shaking."

"I've never been afraid the way I was today," Jo said.

"That's because you can usually see where you are," Pauline said. "I'm always afraid I'll bump into something or fall down, the way I did on your stairs."

"But that was my fault," Jo said. "My foot fell asleep, and I lost my balance."

"It wasn't your fault," Pauline said. "I worry

67

that I'm going to fall and then I fall and then the next time I worry even more."

"So you stay in your room," Jo said. "Where you know where everything is."

"It's better that way," Pauline replied. "My parents prefer it as well. When I'm with them, they're forced to remember that I'm blind. When they don't see me, they don't have to think about me. But they're always traveling, and usually I stay at home with the servants. This time, though, Grandmother and Grandfather invited me to stay with them."

"But you can't just stay in your room forever," Jo said.

"There's nowhere else for me to go," Pauline said. "At least nowhere my parents will allow me to go."

"Where won't they allow you to go?" Jo asked. "Is there someplace you'd like to be?"

Pauline nodded. "There's a school for the blind right in Boston. It's called Perkins. I could be with children there who are just like me. They'd even teach me to read."

"How could you do that?" Jo asked.

"It's a system called Braille," Pauline said. "The governess I had before Miss Johnson told me about it. She even told my parents and said it was a crime they didn't send me to Perkins, so they dismissed her."

"I've never heard of Braille," Jo said. "How does it work?"

"You read the letters through your fingers," Pauline said. "Each letter is made up of dots. I should love to be able to read. You don't know how lucky you are, Jo, that you can."

"You're right," said Jo. "I don't know how lucky I am. Pauline, why won't your parents let you go to that school?"

"Because it's so shameful that I'm blind," she said. "If I went to Perkins, I'd be with other blind people who don't come from nearly as good families as I do."

"But what difference does that make?" Jo asked. "You'd learn how to read. You wouldn't have to sit in a chair all day long, scared to move around."

"Sometimes when I sit in the chair and my governess stops talking, I make up stories,"

Pauline said. "If I had friends, I could tell them my stories, and if I knew Braille, I could write them down."

"You can tell your stories to me," Jo said. "Any time you want."

"Not now," Pauline said. "I'm too tired."

"Me too," Jo said. "But when we wake up, I'll want to hear them all."

"And I want to hear *The Curse of Montevideo,*" Pauline said. "Good night, Jo."

"Good night," Jo said, and fell asleep the moment she closed her eyes.

Something woke Jo a few hours later. When she thought about it, she realized she could no longer hear the wind howling. It was still pitch black, but she cautiously climbed out of the carriage and made her way to the side of the building until she could feel the door. She opened it, afraid of what she might find.

But the snow had stopped, and there was a full moon casting such a bright light that Jo could see a house not too far away. Jo kept the door open and used the moonlight to find her way back to the carriage. "Pauline, wake up," she said.

"What?" Pauline asked. "Where am I? Jo?"

"I'm right here," Jo said. "The snow's stopped, and there's a full moon. I can see a house right near us."

"Do you think they'll let us in?" Pauline asked.

"I'm sure they will," Jo said. "And I'd much rather spend the rest of the night in a house than a carriage."

"I don't know which shoes are mine," Pauline said. "Climb back in here, Jo, and put on yours, so I'll know which ones belong on my feet."

Jo laughed as she climbed back into the carriage. "It must have been a snow squall," she said. "I was afraid it was a blizzard and we'd be stuck in this carriage house forever."

"I think you're the bravest girl I've ever met," Pauline said. "Well, I haven't met many girls, but I think you're probably the bravest girl ever."

"The only reason I was brave was because you were," Jo said. "Pauline, you simply have to go to that school and learn how to read and write."

"But how?" Pauline asked. "Jo, could you tie my shoelaces? I don't know how."

"I'm sure they teach that at the school as well," Jo said. "There are so many reasons why you should be there."

"Oh, Jo," Pauline said. "I would be so happy if that could happen."

"We'll see to it that it does," Jo said. "Oh, I'm sorry, Pauline."

"About what?" Pauline asked.

"I used the word 'see,' " Jo said. "I forgot that I shouldn't."

"There's nothing you can't say to me, Jo," Pauline declared. "Come, let's get out of here."

Jo led Pauline out of the carriage house. The moon shone brightly on them as they began the journey together toward the house.

CHAPTER 9

*A*s Jo and Pauline approached the house, Jo realized that it was Aunt March's. Never had she thought she'd be so happy to pay a call on her difficult great-aunt.

Jo knocked on the door as loudly as she could. She had no idea what time of night it was, but she knew it had to be late, since there were no lights burning.

Eventually Aunt March's butler opened the door. "Miss Josephine," Williams said, obviously startled to see her. "Is there trouble at home?"

"No," Jo said. "This is my friend Pauline.

We need to spend the night here. I don't want to wake Aunt March, but I'm sure she won't mind."

"I'm sure she won't," Williams said. "Come in. Why don't you use the second bedroom upstairs? There's no fire burning, but one of the maids can prepare one."

"Thank you," Jo said. "But that won't be necessary. We'll be fine with blankets and comforters. And we'll explain everything in the morning."

"I look forward to hearing the story," the butler said.

Jo smiled at him. "Come, Pauline," she said. "Hold my hand. And don't swing your arm around. If you break something of Aunt March's, she'll kill me!"

"I'll be careful," Pauline promised, and she stayed close by Jo and kept her arm by her side.

The girls undressed in the second bedroom. There were no nightclothes to change into, but each girl wrapped in a blanket and climbed into the fluffy down-covered bed. Even without a fire, Jo was considerably warmer and more comfortable than she had been in Aunt March's carriage.

Jo woke up first. She got out of bed quietly, careful not to wake Pauline, and made her way downstairs.

"Josephine," Aunt March said. "I heard that you were paying a surprise visit."

"As much a surprise to me as you, Aunt March," Jo said. "Thank you for your hospitality last night."

"You're most welcome," Aunt March said. "Sit down, child, and tell me what happened."

Jo accepted her aunt's invitation. "Pauline was unhappy at our house," she said. "Uncomfortable and scared. She wanted to go back to her grandparents, and I said I'd take her. Only on the way, we got caught in the snow squall. Aunt March, I was so frightened. But Pauline and I found your carriage house. We didn't know it was yours, but we let ourselves in, and we slept in your carriage, and then when the squall ended I could see your house and we came here. Pauline's still asleep upstairs. No one will be worried about us, because the Wheelers think Pauline's at our house and Marmee and Father think I'm here. I told Meg I might spend the night here if it was too dark to go home."

"That's quite a story," said Aunt March. "Are you sure Pauline is all right?"

"Yes, Aunt March," Jo said. "But no, not really. I don't mean she's sick or anything like that. But she's so desperately unhappy."

"It's a great tragedy to be blind," said Aunt March.

"I suppose it is," Jo said. "But it seems to me that her parents are making it a greater tragedy than it needs to be."

"And what do you mean by that?" Aunt March asked.

"There's a school Pauline could go to," Jo said. "Right in Boston. And her parents know about it, but they don't want to send her there."

"I'm sure they have their reasons," Aunt March said.

"It's because they think only poor people attend Perkins," Jo said. "It's a school where Pauline could learn to read and write and take care of herself. Aunt March, Pauline doesn't even know how to tie her shoelaces. And she's terrified of leaving her home and going anywhere she's never been before. What kind of life is that for her? She's smart and brave, and she should have a chance to meet people and read and just be a normal girl who can't see, instead of some poor helpless blind person."

"I'm sure her parents want what's best for her," Aunt March said.

"Are you?" Jo asked. "Because I'm not sure of that at all. I think they're ashamed of Pauline and just as happy to keep her locked up like some sort of pet. They think as long as she's clean and well fed, that's all she needs. Well, it isn't. She needs more. Any person would."

Aunt March stared at Jo, who felt herself turn red. She'd never spoken that way to Aunt March before and could hardly imagine what the old woman would make of it.

But Aunt March surprised her. "I think you

might be right," she said. "You say this school could teach Pauline to read and write? Even though she's blind?"

"Pauline told me about it last night," Jo said. "They use some kind of special system where you read the words through your fingers. I've forgotten what Pauline called it."

"That makes a great deal of sense," Aunt March said. "I believe I've heard of Perkins, but I'm not very familiar with its reputation or methods. Is it a respectable school?"

"I'm sure it is," Jo said.

"And you say Pauline is intelligent?" Aunt March asked. "She isn't slow-witted?"

"Not at all," said Jo. "If she had a chance to learn, to really learn, Aunt March, I think she'd be as smart as anyone I know."

"Then we must see to it she has that chance," said Aunt March. "I don't believe in wasting what God has given us. Come, Josephine. Let's rouse Pauline, and speak to her grandparents about her future."

Pauline was already awake when Jo went

upstairs to fetch her. Jo helped Pauline dress, and they joined Aunt March in the parlor.

"We'll take the carriage to your grand-parents'," said Aunt March. "The one you used as a bed last night. And I intend to speak to them."

Jo grinned. Aunt March usually addressed Jo in that tone, so it was a pleasure to know that someone else was going to feel Aunt March's righteous wrath.

The Wheelers were surprised to see Pauline, Jo, and Aunt March at their door so early on a Sunday morning. "Is everything all right?" Mrs. Wheeler asked as they warmed them-selves by the parlor fireplace.

"In some senses, yes," said Aunt March. "And in others, no."

"I don't understand," said Mr. Wheeler. He was a tall, imposing man, and Jo was glad Aunt March was there to fight this battle with her.

"Pauline and Josephine had a bit of an ad-venture last night," said Aunt March. "I'm sure Pauline will tell you all about it later. I am here to discuss something far more important, and that is Pauline's future."

"My future?" Pauline asked.

"Your future as an educated young woman of Massachusetts," Aunt March said. "It has come to my attention that there is a school for the blind in Boston. I fail to see why Pauline has not been sent there."

"Her parents are opposed to it," Mrs. Wheeler said.

"Parents do not always know what is best for their children," Aunt March said. "There have been many occasions when I have found it necessary to discuss with Josephine's parents the best way of raising her."

Jo tried not to smile.

"Pauline should learn how to read and write and tie her own shoelaces," Aunt March said. "And if this school can teach her those things, it is a sin for her not to be sent there."

"And you would have us send her there without her parents' consent?" Mr. Wheeler asked.

"My understanding is that they won't be back for months," Aunt March said. "Months that Pauline can spend learning valuable things. If her parents insist on removing her from the school when they return, at least by then she will have learned some basic lessons."

"Is that what you want, Pauline?" Mrs. Wheeler asked.

"Oh, yes," Pauline said. "I want so much to be able to read and write and learn how to get around. I don't want to be helpless my whole life. I want to be more like Jo."

"I never thought I'd say this," Aunt March declared, "but there is a great deal to be said for being more like Jo."

And much to Jo's delight, everyone laughed.

CHAPTER 10

"Jo, there's a letter for you," Marmee said one warm day in May.

"A letter for me?" Jo said. "Who is it from?"

"Open it and find out," Meg said.

"Yes, open it," Amy demanded. "None of us ever gets a letter."

"I'm sure it's something wonderful," said Beth. "Do open it, Jo."

"Give me a chance," Jo muttered. She broke open the seal and took the letter out of its envelope.

"Who is it from?" Meg asked.

"Pauline," Jo said, turning to the last page to read the signature.

"Read it to us," Amy said.

"Only the parts you think she'd want us to know," said Beth.

"I'm sure she won't mind if I read it all to you," said Jo. "She liked all of you nearly as much as she liked me."

"I would like to hear the letter also," Marmee said. "If you think Pauline liked me as well."

"She liked you the best, I'm sure," Jo said. "All right. This is what Pauline has to say: 'Dear Jo, This is Pauline writing to you. Actually, I'm not doing the writing. One of my teachers is writing for me. I wrote this letter in Braille first—' "

"What's Braille?" Amy asked.

"It's a way for blind people to read and write," Jo said. "Pauline told me about it before she left for school.

" 'I wrote this letter in Braille first,' " Jo continued, " 'and my teacher is transcribing it for you to read. She says I am the fastest student in Braille she has ever known. I told her it was because there were so many things I've wanted to read. Of course there aren't many books published in Braille yet, because they are very expensive to produce. But I have decided to use my money to get more books written in Braille. This will be my life's work.' "

"That's so good of her," said Beth.

"It is," said Jo. "Of course, that way there'll be more for her to read as well." She resumed the letter.

" 'This will be my life's work. Of course, the more books there are in Braille, the more I'll have to read.' " Jo smiled. " 'In Braille,' " she continued, " 'each letter of the alphabet is made up of a different series of dots. The next time I visit my grandparents, I'll show you how it's done.' "

"That will be fun," said Jo. "Think how it must be to read through your fingertips."

"Don't interrupt," Amy said. "Keep reading."

It was just like Amy to say that, Jo thought, but she went back to the letter instead of objecting.

" 'I can read the Bible now, instead of having it read to me. And I'm translating poems I know by heart into Braille so that the other children here can read them as well. It is hard work, but I feel so proud of myself for all I've mastered. Oh, Jo, I can tie my own shoelaces now!' "

"Pauline couldn't tie her own laces?" Amy asked.

"Who's interrupting now?" Jo asked.

"But I've been able to tie my own laces for years," said Amy.

"But you're not blind, and you don't have a maid to tie them for you," Meg said. "Go back to the letter, Jo."

" 'Oh, Jo, I can tie my own shoelaces now!' " Jo repeated. " 'And I've learned how to dress on my own. Sometimes I have trouble with buttons, but of course when I go home I'll have a maid to help. Still, it's a wonderful feeling to be able to dress myself the way you and your sisters can.' "

"I'd rather have a maid," Amy muttered.

Jo rolled her eyes. " '. . . dress myself the way you and your sisters can,' " she read again. " 'And remember how I used to walk, with my arms flailing about as I tried to feel what was around me, and how I used to knock things over?' "

"I remember," Meg said with a shudder.

" 'Now I have a cane,' " Jo read. " 'Not a heavy walking stick. More like a branch that I carry and use to find things so that I won't bump into them. The first few weeks here, I had a lot of trouble with it, and I still do bump into things on occasion, but it's a great improvement. And the other children here have sticks like mine, and you can hear all of us tap-tap-tapping as we walk down the corridors. It's a comforting sound somehow.' "

"I should like to try that," Beth said. "Walking with my eyes closed, using a stick to guide myself."

"We could all try it," Meg said. "And then we'd know better what Pauline goes through."

"You'll never let me finish this letter, will you?" Jo moaned.

"I'm sorry," Beth said.

" 'Are your sisters there with you?' " Jo read. " 'I hope they are. I was so envious of you, Jo, having such wonderful sisters. I wish I loved mine as you love yours. My parents wrote to my grandparents and told them they have found a husband for one of my sisters, but that the other one is turning down every man she meets. Of course, they intend to stay until my one sister is married. The wedding is scheduled for next October. Perhaps by then they'll find a husband for my other sister as well.' "

Jo lowered the letter. "This is terrible of me," she said. "But I hope it takes them forever." Her sisters and Marmee nodded.

" 'This is terrible of me,' " Jo read. " 'But I hope it takes them a long, long time.' "

Jo's sisters laughed. "A long, long time is a bit better than forever," Meg said.

" '. . . a long, long time. My grandparents wrote to tell them I was in school, and my mother wrote back to say they couldn't be bothered with such things now. They would deal with my situation after the wedding and after they found someone for my other sister to marry.' "

Marmee shook her head. "I know I shouldn't speak ill of others," she said, "but people like that should not be permitted to have children."

"Marmee!" Meg said.

"Forgive me," Marmee said. "But they make me so angry."

"You should have seen Aunt March," Jo said.

"Jo, can you finish the letter?" Amy asked.

" 'It makes me so happy to think I'll be here at least a few more months,' " Jo read. " 'I'm trying to learn as much as I can as fast as I can in case my parents insist I leave when they get back. Of course, I'm hoping they'll let me stay. When they see how happy I am and how little I need them, they might think it's best for me here. But I can't be sure of that, so the more I learn now, the safer I'll be. And Jo, I've made friends! Real friends. We laugh together and talk about all sorts of things, and we practice reading aloud to each other. I never knew it could be such fun to have friends. When I see you next, Jo, I'll tell you about all of them. Most of them are poor, as my parents feared, but that doesn't seem to matter here."

"It shouldn't matter anywhere," Marmee said. "But I'm afraid it will take a while before the world realizes that."

" 'You'll hardly know me when I visit my grandparents,' " Jo read. " 'I won't be that disagreeable scared girl you first met. I want to go on walks with you, Jo, and smell the flowers and feel the sun on my face. I want to play with you and your sisters and be in the audience for *The Curse of Montevideo*. I'm not sure how to spell that, but you know what I mean. And I most especially want to call on your great-aunt and tell her how wonderful she is, and how much I owe her.' "

"Aunt March will like that," Amy said.

"She deserves it," Jo said. "None of this would have happened if it hadn't been for Aunt March."

Meg laughed. "Do you remember when we talked about why Pauline was blind?" she asked. "And you said, Marmee, that maybe it would change Jo for the better? I think it must have. I've never heard her say anything nice about Aunt March before."

"She hasn't deserved it before," Jo said. "Will you please let me finish this letter?"

"I'm sorry," Meg said, but she didn't look the least bit sorry.

" 'Jo, I never knew I could be so happy. I think about you all the time and how much you did for me. Please give my warmest regards to your sisters and your parents and your aunt. I remain, most truly, your friend, Pauline.' "

"Pauline is going to do great good," Jo said. "She's going to learn so much, and then she's going to help others who share her problem. I know that, Marmee, even if I can't tell the future."

Marmee smiled. "Sometimes the future can be guessed at," she said. "And I believe you're right, Jo, dear. Thanks to you, Pauline's future is bright indeed."

Jo looked at her mother and sisters. She didn't know what her future would be, but she decided then and there that she would try to help as many other people as she could.

And she smiled at the thought.

PORTRAITS OF
LITTLE WOMEN
ACTIVITIES

APPLE-DAPPLE LOAF

This delicious, cakelike bread can be served plain at breakfast or lunch. A scoop of warm applesauce or your favorite ice cream makes it an extra-special dessert.

INGREDIENTS

1/4 cup butter or margarine, melted and cooled

2/3 cup sugar

2 eggs

2 cups all-purpose flour

1 teaspoon baking powder

1 teaspoon baking soda

1 teaspoon salt

2 cups peeled, coarsely grated raw apple

(Granny Smith or Golden Delicious is
    best; try using a cup of each)
½ cup chopped walnuts or pecans

Preheat oven to 350 degrees.
Grease and flour a 9-by-5-by-3-inch loaf
pan.

1. Beat butter, sugar and eggs together in
   a bowl until light and fluffy.
2. In another bowl, sift together dry
   ingredients.
3. To butter mixture, alternately add dry
   ingredients and grated apples, mixing
   well after each addition.
4. Add nuts. Mixture will be stiff.
5. Spoon batter into greased and floured
   pan.
6. Bake about 1 hour, or until a cake
   tester inserted into center of loaf comes
   out barely dry. Be careful not to
   overbake.

Cool completely, then turn loaf out onto
plate to serve. Don't forget that a slice tastes
perfect morning, noon, or night.

SPECIAL MOMENTS SCRAPBOOK

Memories . . . This little book is perfect for recording the many special moments in your life.

MATERIALS

12 brown paper lunch bags
Hole puncher
½ yard twine or narrow ribbon
White glue
Pen
Photographs, stickers, postcards, artificial flowers, or any other decorations you like
Extra twine or ribbon (optional)

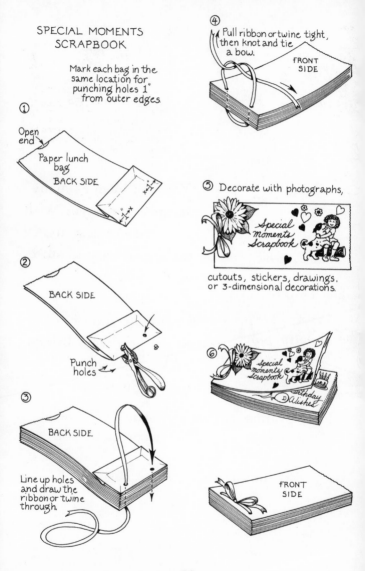

SPECIAL MOMENTS SCRAPBOOK

Mark each bag in the same location for punching holes 1" from outer edges.

① Open end
Paper lunch bag
BACK SIDE

② BACK SIDE
Punch holes

③ BACK SIDE
Line up holes and draw the ribbon or twine through.

④ Pull ribbon or twine tight, then knot and tie a bow.
FRONT SIDE

⑤ Decorate with photographs,
Special moments scrapbook
cutouts, stickers, drawings, or 3-dimensional decorations.

⑥ special moments scrapbook
birthday wishes

FRONT SIDE

e.g.

Camping with my cousins

Summer Vacation

⑩

My "Best" Friends

Use twine or ribbon and hole puncher at the open end to keep your mementos safe and private.

In each bag you can save mementos such as notes, cards, tickets, and other reminders of special events.

You can have as many scrapbooks as you wish . . . they're easy to make and easy to store. And you'll soon discover that a scrapbook full of treasures always brings back memories of special times.

ABOUT THE AUTHOR OF
PORTRAITS OF LITTLE WOMEN

SUSAN BETH PFEFFER is the author of both middle-grade and young adult fiction. Her middle-grade novels include *Nobody's Daughter* and its companion, *Justice for Emily*. Her highly praised *The Year Without Michael* is an ALA Best Book for Young Adults, an ALA YALSA Best of the Best, and a *Publishers Weekly* Best Book of the Year. Her novels for young adults include *Twice Taken, Most Precious Blood, About David*, and *Family of Strangers*. Susan Beth Pfeffer lives in Middletown, New York.

A WORD ABOUT
LOUISA MAY ALCOTT

LOUISA MAY ALCOTT was born in 1832 in Germantown, Pennsylvania, and grew up in the Boston-Concord area of Massachusetts. She received her early education from her father, Bronson Alcott, a renowned educator and writer, who eventually left teaching to study philosophy. To supplement the family income, Louisa worked as a teacher, a household servant, and a seamstress, and she wrote stories as well as poems for newspapers and magazines. In 1868 she published the first volume of *Little Women,* a novel about four sisters growing up in a small New England town during the Civil War. The immediate success of *Little Women* made Louisa May Alcott a celebrated writer, and the novel remains one of today's best-loved books. Alcott wrote until her death in 1888.